To Nikoi

Bullying is not cool!

Mark Kato

LOUKOUMI
And The Schoolyard Bully

Nick Katsoris

For a Cause

A minimum of $2 from the sale of each book will be donated to:

St. Jude Children's
Research Hospital
ALSAC • Danny Thomas, Founder
Finding cures. Saving children.

St. Jude Children's Research Hospital® is the global leader in finding cures and saving children from cancer and other deadly diseases. St. Jude freely shares discoveries they make and every child saved at St. Jude means doctors and scientists can use that knowledge to save thousands more children around the world. Unlike any other hospital, St. Jude relies on funding from the general public. Thanks to its generous donors, families never receive a bill from St. Jude for treatment, travel, housing or food. For more information, please visit **stjude.org**.

"The Loukoumi book series has long been a friend to children, opening their eyes to the world around them. This time, it provides comfort and assurance to kids who are frightened and bewildered by bullying. A worthy subject. We at St. Jude Children's Research Hospital are honored to be beneficiaries of such a noble project."

**–Marlo Thomas, National Outreach Director
St. Jude Children's Research Hospital**

Nia
Vardalos

Narrated by Nia Vardalos
Academy Award and Golden Globe nominated Actress
and screenwriter of *My Big Fat Greek Wedding*;
Author of the bestselling book, *Instant Mom*.

Featuring Academy Award Winner Morgan Freeman
as Igor the alligator

and the character voices of:
John Aniston • Alexis Christoforous • Frank Dicopoulos
Academy Award Winner Olympia Dukakis
Grammy Award Winner Gloria Gaynor and Constantine Maroulis

Morgan
Freeman

Dedication

To all the children of the world, embrace your individuality, and respect the differences in others. You may be different, but you are really all the same.
To Nia Vardalos, thank you for your amazing narration and your friendship.
To Morgan Freeman for wonderfully bringing the character of Igor the alligator to life, and as always to Voula, Dean and Julia for making it all worthwhile!
— Nick Katsoris

Special thanks to: John Aniston, Alexis Christoforous, Frank Dicopoulos, Olympia Dukakis, Gloria Gaynor and Constantine Maroulis for wonderfully reprising their character voices in the *Loukoumi And The Schoolyard Bully* audio book. Congratulations to Caila Tsamutalis, the winner of our Loukoumi Illustration Contest, for inspiring the illustration of Oinkerella the pig on page five of this book, and to all the contest finalists (George, Victoria, Eleni, Caila, Marina, Amanda, Georgia, Renzo, Aryetta and Kara Lynn), whose illustrations are pictured in order below.

Loukoumi entered the schoolyard with a huge smile on her face. She couldn't wait to tell her friends some exciting news!

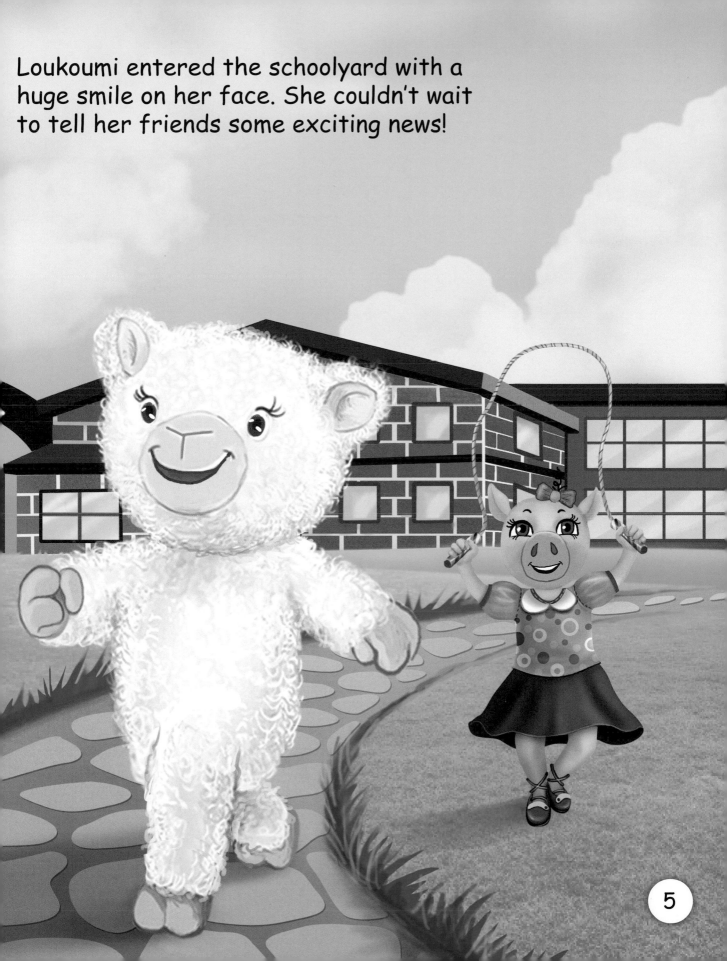

"Guess what?" Loukoumi called out.
"I am going to have a baby brother!"

"That's great!" Marika said.

"Wow! What are we going to name him?"
Dean asked, shaking his tail with excitement.

"How about Fistiki Junior?" Fistiki chuckled.

Before Loukoumi had a chance to answer,
Igor the alligator interrupted.

Loukoumi was scared of Igor. He was
much taller than Loukoumi and always
pushed everyone around the schoolyard.

"With a name like Loukoumi," Igor said, "I can just imagine what your parents are going to call the *next* lamb!"

"Igor, my name is a Greek word that means *sweet*, and Loukoumi is a type of candy - a jelly candy with powdered sugar all over it," Loukoumi said.

"Really!" Igor said. "Then you need some powdered sugar on you," throwing dirt all over Loukoumi.

"Hey, pick on someone your own size!" Fistiki said, holding his fists up in the air.

"I enjoy picking on Loukoumi, or should I call her Loukoumoumou. That's what you should name your brother, Loukoumoumou!" Igor said, as others in the schoolyard laughed.

"Or how about Loucoconut?" He continued,
and then walked away.

"Don't let him bother you Loukoumi,"
Dean said, as Marika dusted the dirt from
Loukoumi's fur. "He's just a big bully!"

"I know," Loukoumi said in a sad voice, "but it still hurts."

"You should be proud of your name!" Marika said. "Everyone is different, yet we're really all the same. You shouldn't make fun of someone, especially their name. You shouldn't be a bully because it really isn't cool. You should be accepting of others. That's the golden rule."

"You guys are the best friends," Loukoumi said.

The school bell rang and everyone proceeded to math class where Loukoumi sits next to Igor every day.

As they were taking notes, Igor's pencil broke.

Loukoumi, could you please give Igor one of your extra pencils?" Professor Gus said.

Thanks, um...Loukoumi," Igor said, taking the pencil out of Loukoumi's hands.

17

Later that morning, it was time for gym class. The students were playing basketball, one of Loukoumi's favorite sports!

"Let's go team!" Professor Gus said.

Igor neared the net. Loukoumi passed the ball. Igor shot and scored!

"Nice pass!" Igor said, wondering why Loukoumi passed the ball to him.

19

Next on the schedule was lunch. As the students entered the cafeteria, Fistiki's tummy was growling.

Loukoumi was eating her grilled cheese sandwich. She then discovered a box of Loukoumi candy in her lunchbox that her parents packed for her as a surprise. Loukoumi was so excited!

Loukoumi opened up the box of Loukoumi candy and offered a piece to all her friends.

"This is tasty!" Fistiki said, with powdered sugar all over his mouth.

23

When Loukoumi got to Igor, she paused. He was looking at her differently than he did earlier that morning.

"Here is a piece of Loukoumi candy for you too, Igor," Loukoumi said. "You do like candy, right?"

"Everybody likes candy!" Igor said. "I guess we are more alike than I thought. You know, Loukoumi is the perfect name for you because you really are *sweet*. I'm sorry, Loukoumi, for making fun of you earlier today."

"Thanks, Igor!" Loukoumi said. "It really is cooler to be nice."

"You're right, Loukoumi!" Igor agreed.
"Everyone is different, yet we're really all the same.
I shouldn't make fun of someone, especially their name.
I won't be a bully, because it really isn't cool.
I will be accepting of others. That's my golden rule."

Several weeks later, Loukoumi's brother was born and Loukoumi went to the hospital to meet him.

"He's so cute!" Loukoumi said. "What are we going to name him?"

Loukoumi's Dad put his arm around Loukoumi, gave her a kiss on the head, and said, "Loukoumi, we are so blessed to have you in our lives, and we want your baby brother to be just as sweet as you."

"You're going to name him Loukoumi?" she questioned.

"Well, we can't call him Loukoumi too," her Dad answered, "but we can name him Lou."

"I like that!" Loukoumi said. "Baby Lou."

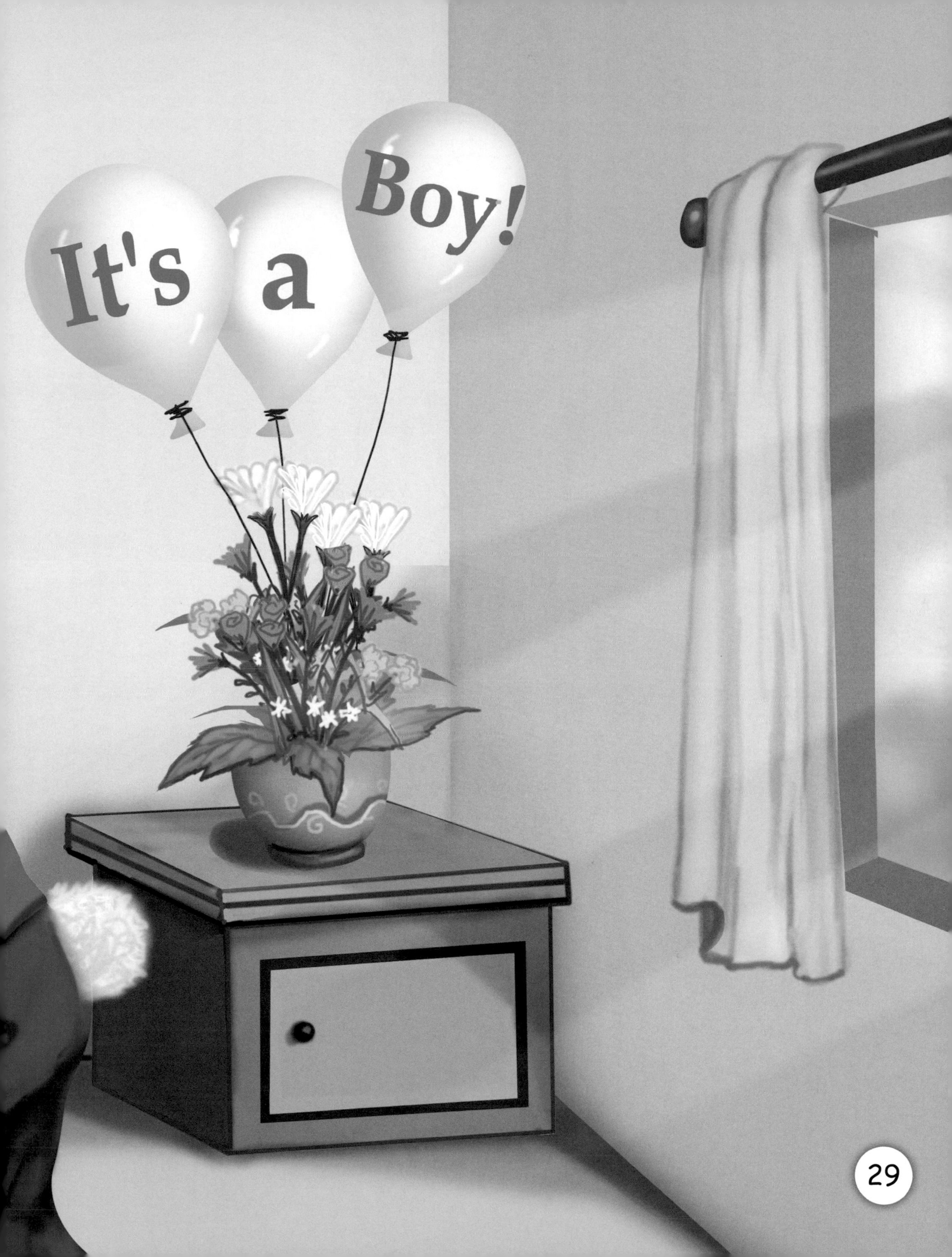
It's
a
Boy!

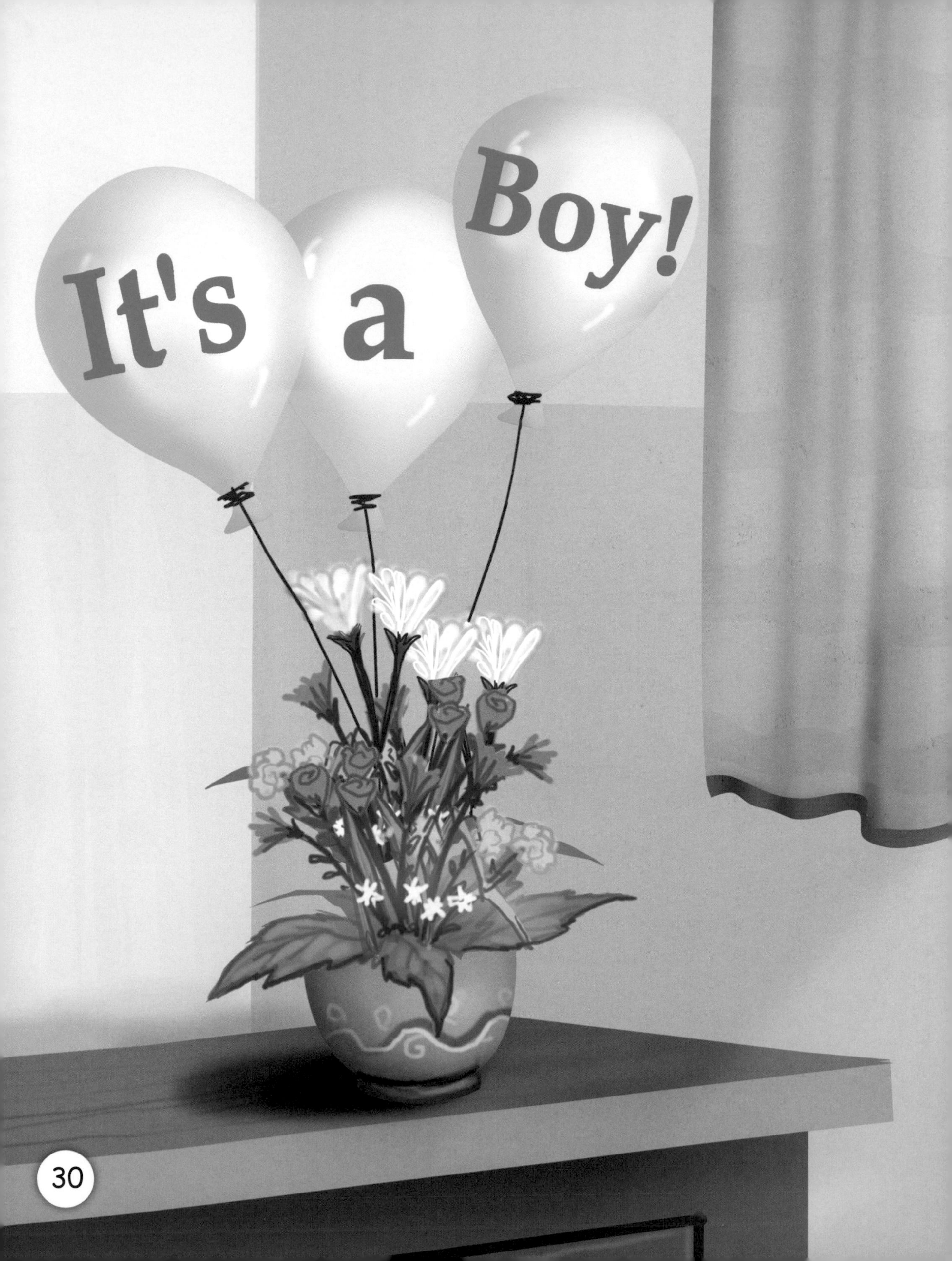
It's
a
Boy!

Loukoumi kissed her new brother on the forehead, and said, "I love you baby Lou. I promise to be the best big sister. We are going to have so much fun together. I'm going to protect you, and be there for you, and I can't wait to share my Loukoumi candy with you too!"

THE END

31

About the Author

Loukoumi And The Schoolyard Bully is Nick Katsoris' 6th book in the Loukoumi series. Other titles include the iParenting Media Award winning: *Loukoumi, Growing Up With Loukoumi, Loukoumi's Good Deeds, Loukoumi's Gift* and *Loukoumi's Celebrity Cookbook.* The books also have been translated into Greek. Katsoris sponsors the *Growing Up With Loukoumi Dream Day* contest, which grants kids the opportunity to spend the day in their dream careers. He also sponsors *Make A Difference With Loukoumi Day,* based on his book *Loukoumi's Good Deeds* (narrated on CD by Jennifer Aniston and John Aniston), which rallies thousands of kids each October to do a good deed on *National Make A Difference Day.* In addition, the winner of the *Loukoumi's Celebrity Cookbook* Recipe Contest, Grace LaFountain, cooked her favorite childhood recipe with Celebrity Chef Cat Cora at Cat's restaurant, Kouzzina, on the BoardWalk in Walt Disney World during the 2012 Epcot Food and Wine Festival. Katsoris is a New York attorney as General Counsel of the Red Apple Group, and President of the Hellenic Times Scholarship Fund, which has awarded over 850 scholarships totaling over $2 million. Nick is also a board member of Chefs For Humanity, has worked on a Loukoumi literacy awareness program with the National Ladies Philoptochos Society, and is a member of Kiwanis International, where he was the keynote speaker at their international convention's Faith and Humor breakfast in Vancouver, Canada. Nick is also author of the legal thriller *Crimes of Fire.* He currently resides in Eastchester, New York, with his wife, Voula, a real estate attorney, and their children, Dean and Julia.

Photo by Jillian Nelson

Loukoumi's Celebrity Cookbook
Featuring Favorite Childhood Recipes By Over 50 Celebrities

- *Great Ideas!* —**PEOPLE Magazine**
- *A fun, nostalgic cookbook!* —**OPRAH.com**
- *A new fave!* —**PARADE Magazine**
- *Star-studded recipes that benefit a great cause!* —**USA WEEKEND Magazine**
- *Recipes that make celebrities feel like a kid again!* —**ABC-TV's The VIEW**
- *A Wonderful Cookbook! Fabulous!* —**Better TV**
- *Loukoumi's Celebrity Cookbook will give you a chance to cook with your kids and teach them about helping those in need.* —**PARENTS Magazine**
- *A Great Little Book! Encourages kids to get into the kitchen!* —**Good Day NY**
- *A whimsical recipe project.* —**FOX News**
- *Communities of all kinds put together favorite recipe compilations, and although this book features a celebrity community, there's a similar quaintness to it.* —**School Library Journal**
- *Loukoumi learns the importance of never giving up.* —**Disney's FAMILY FUN Magazine**
- *One of the Best New Parenting Books!* —**SCHOLASTIC PARENT & CHILD MAGAZINE**
- *Over 50 stars share their favorite childhood recipes!* —**Entertainment Tonight**

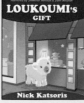